RHUMBA

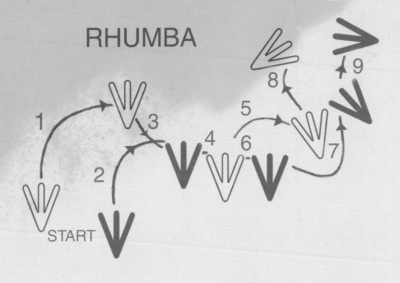

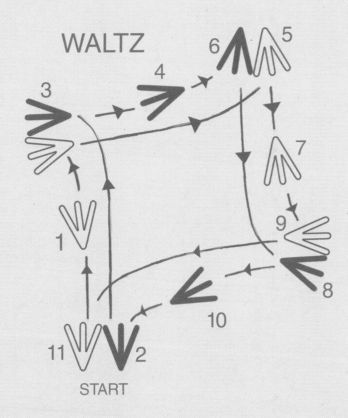

WALTZ

STERLING CHILDREN'S BOOKS
New York

An Imprint of Sterling Publishing
1166 Avenue of the Americas
New York, NY 10036

Text © 2009 by Tammi Sauer
Illustrations © 2009 by Dan Santat
The illustrations in this book were created using acrylic and ink with Adobe PhotoSho

Designed by Kate Moll and Dan Santat

Paperback edition published in 2015.
Previously published by Sterling Publishing, Co., Inc. in a different format in 2009.

ISBN 978-1-4549-1477-8

Library of Congress Cataloging-in-Publication Data

Sauer, Tammi.
  Chicken dance / by Tammi Sauer ; illustrated by Dan Santat.
    p. cm.
  Summary: Determined to win tickets to an Elvis Poultry concert,
hens Marge and Lola enter the Barnyard Talent Show, then, while the
ducks who usually win the contest jeer, they test out their abilities.
  ISBN 978-1-4027-5366-4
  [1. Talent shows--Fiction. 2. Ability--Fiction. 3. Chickens--Fiction.
4. Domestic animals--Fiction. 5. Humorous stories.] I. Santat, Dan, ill. II. Titl
  PZ7.S2502Chi 2009
  [E]--dc22   2008050578

Distributed in Canada by Sterling Publishing
C/o Canadian Manda Group, 664 Annette Street
Toronto, Ontario, Canada M6S 2C8
Distributed in the United Kingdom by GMC Distribution Services
Castle Place, 166 High Street, Lewes, East Sussex, England BN7 1XU
Distributed in Australia by Capricorn Link (Australia) Pty. Ltd.
P.O. Box 704, Windsor, NSW 2756, Australia

For information about custom editions, special sales, and premium
and corporate purchases, please contact Sterling Special Sales at 800-805-5489
or specialsales@sterlingpublishing.com.

Manufactured in China
Lot #:
2 4 6 8 10 9 7 5 3 1
01/15

www.sterlingpublishing.com/kids

STEREO

presented in HI-FIDELITY

CHICKEN DANCE

written by **TAMMI SAUER**

illustrated by **DAN SANTAT**

STERLING CHILDREN'S BOOKS

New York

FOR MY MOM, RAMONA KIPPES, WHO TOTALLY BAWKS AND ROLLS. -T.S.

FOR LEAH, ALEK, AND KYLE. - D.S.

TONIGHT
BARNYARD
TALENT
SHOW
GRAND PRIZE
TICKETS TO....
ELVIS
POULTRY
IN CONCERT
THE FINAL DOODLE DOO

Marge and Lola took one look at the poster on the barn door and almost lost their cluck. Elvis Poultry was *top bird.* They had to win those tickets.

The ducks paraded by.
"Don't bother, drumsticks."
"Ducks win every year."
"All a chicken can do is bawk, flap, and shake."
Marge and Lola ignored the quackers and tested
out their talents.

Bowling was out.

So was juggling.

And tightrope walking.

"We could try flying," Marge said.
Lola grinned. "Flying chickens?
Now that's talent!"
The chickens scrambled to the top
of the coop.

They **jumped.**

They **fluttered.**

They sank in hay up to their wattles.
The ducks flew by.
"Bail out, chickens!" they called down below.

Marge and Lola dusted themselves off and shook hay
from their feathers.
"Now what?" asked Lola.
"We could try swimming," said Marge.
Lola nodded. "Swimming chickens? Now that's talent!"

The chickens tottered
to the pond.

They
jumped.

They
fluttered.

They totally sank.

The ducks swam by.
"Get some floaties, chickens!"

Marge and Lola waded ashore and spit water from their beaks.

"Any other big ideas?" asked Lola.

Marge stared at the setting sun. "Too late. It's show time.
We'll have to wing it."

The chickens bumbled to the barn, found their seats, and
settled in for the show.

The goats ate a tractor and scored a seven.
"Not bad," said Marge.

The pigs formed a pyramid and scored an eight.

The cows jumped over the moon.

"That's old!" said Lola. "We can still win this thing!"
Suddenly, trumpets sounded.

The crowd gasped.
The ducks grabbed their boards and hit the water.

They scored . . .

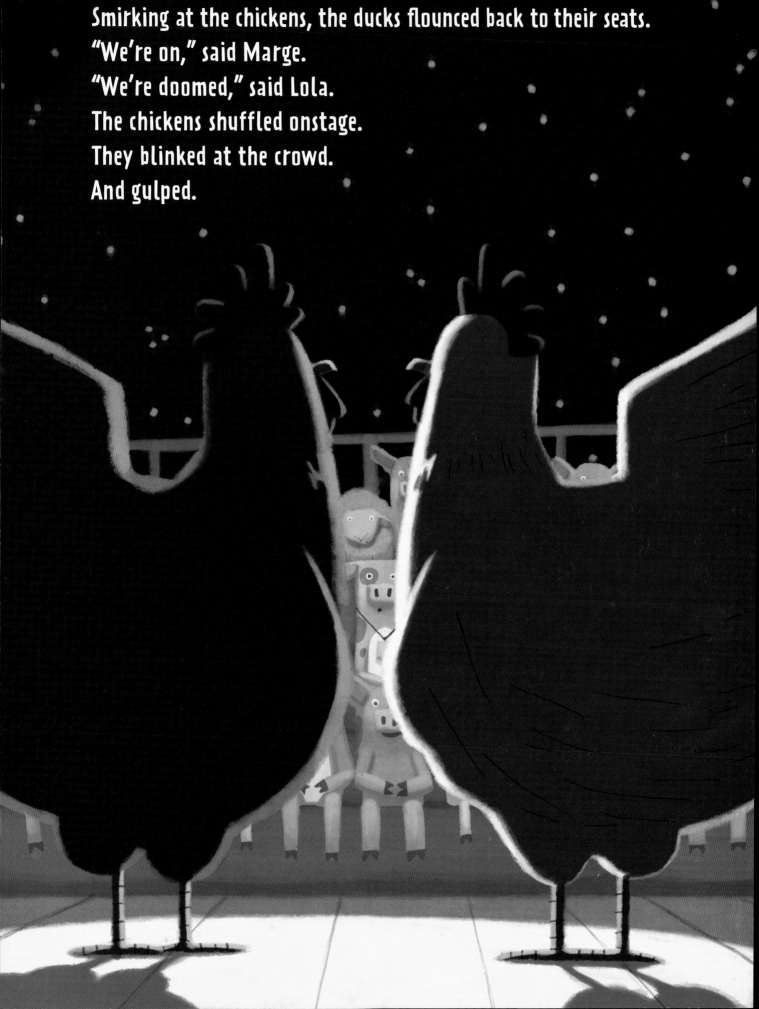

Smirking at the chickens, the ducks flounced back to their seats.

"We're on," said Marge.

"We're doomed," said Lola.

The chickens shuffled onstage.

They blinked at the crowd.

And gulped.

"What's the matter?" yelled a duck.

"Are you chicken?"

This put the chickens in a foul mood.

They BAWKED. They FLAPPED. They SHOOK.

"**More! More! More!**"
the crowd chanted.

Marge and Lola looked at each other.
"But we're just doing regular chicken stuff," Marge whispered.
"Regular chicken stuff? Now *that's* talent!" Lola grabbed a mike.
"Let's bawk and roll!"

The chickens **BAWKED**
and **FLAPPED** and
SHOOK all over the stage.

They scored . . .

. . . an eight-point five.

8.5

8.5

8.5

8.5

"Losers!" the ducks called as they plucked the tickets from the prize table. "Ducks rule."

Marge and Lola gazed at the tickets and wiped their eyes.
Then, from the top of the barn, a voice crooned—
"You chicks rocked!"
A rooster swooped to the stage. "You had me all shook up."

Elvis smoothed his crest. "I could use an act like yours."
Before Marge and Lola could say a word, duck feathers flew.
The ducks lunged at the chickens when—

—the cows came home, scoring a perfect ten.

The next day, a new poster was tacked
on every barn in the countryside . . .

DISCO CHICKEN

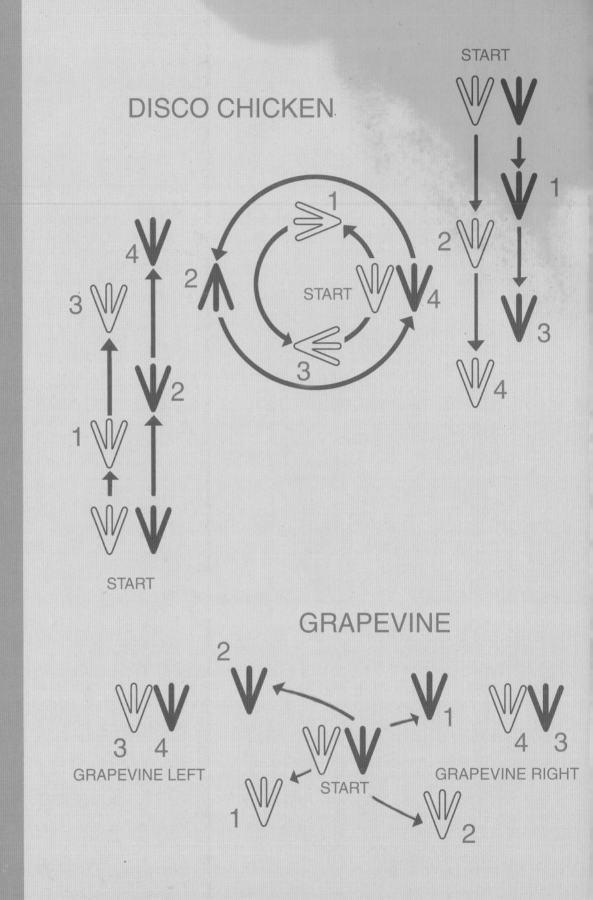

START

4

3

1

2

START

START

1

2

3

4

START

2

4

3

START

GRAPEVINE

2

3 4

GRAPEVINE LEFT

1

1

4 3

GRAPEVINE RIGHT

START

1

2